The REINDEER vs E.A.Ster

A fun, easy Springtime tradition

By Elizabeth Passo
Illustrated by Jon Carraher

Trenton, Bryce, and Grady
You can make a difference!
Elizabeth Passo
2017

Happy Knack Publishing, LLC

www.happyknack.net
Milroy, Pennsylvania

Happy Knack Publishing, LLC
70 Squirrel Hill
Milroy, PA 17063
Phone: (717) 903-6154

We'd love to hear from you!
Email: contact@reindeergift.com
Web: www.happyknack.net
       www.reindeergift.com
       www.elizabethpasso.com

QUANTITY SALES
Discounts are available on bulk purchases. For details, please contact Happy Knack Publishing, LLC.

First Edition

ISBN 978-0-9894968-1-0

Printed in China

Dasher
THE SCHOLAR

Likes:	Reading, thinking up new ideas
Favorite Food:	Crispy grilled cheese sandwich
Favorite Color:	Sophisticated, soothing grey
Favorite Place:	The Reindeer Research Library
Birthday:	February 16

Dancer
THE CHARMER

Likes:	Dancing, baking, friendliness
Favorite Food:	Warm, fresh cookies
Favorite Color:	Graceful, sweet pink
Favorite Place:	The Ravenous Reindeer Cafe
Birthday:	January 11

Prancer
THE MUSICIAN

Likes:	Music, movies, classic style
Favorite Food:	Cheesecake
Favorite Color:	Poised, prosperous green
Favorite Place:	The Reindeer Recording Studio
Birthday:	September 30

Vixen
THE ROCK STAR

Likes: Singing, performing, honesty
Favorite Food: Tacos
Favorite Color: Theatrical, feisty purple
Favorite Place: The Reindeer Performance Stage
Birthday: July 27

Comet
THE FASTEST

Likes: Running, swimming, games
Favorite Food: French fries
Favorite Color: Courageous, radiant yellow
Favorite Place: The Racing Reindeer Track
Birthday: November 28

Cupid
THE ARTIST

Likes: Art, nature, hiking, hugs
Favorite Food: Ice cream
Favorite Color: Warm, affectionate red
Favorite Place: The Reindeer Relaxation Forest
Birthday: March 4

Donner
THE SPORTS STAR

Likes: Sports, strength, fitness
Favorite Food: Pizza
Favorite Color: Reach for the sky, bold blue
Favorite Place: The Robust Reindeer Gym
Birthday: October 25

Blitzen
THE EXPLORER

Likes: Trying new things, science,
                  medicine, gardening, yoga
Favorite Food: Pasta
Favorite Color: Independent, spirited orange
Favorite Place: The Reindeer Roots Garden
Birthday: April 28

E.A.Ster
THE OPTIMIST

Likes: Feeling and spreading joy,
                  rainbows, versatility
Favorite Food: Fluffy pancakes
Favorite Color: Successful, divine gold
Favorite Place: Sunny Bunny Park
Birthday: May 2

On one spectacular sunny Spring day,
The reindeer were taking a rest from their play.
Ever since Christmas, they'd felt pretty frisky
From their gift hiding so daring and risky.

Dasher, who's quick brain is never at rest,
Has ideas everyone thinks are the best.
"Playing that prank on Santa was funny,
So why not play it on E.A.Ster bunny?"

Wait! Stop right there! Dasher said who?
E.A.Ster bunny? That's something that's new.
You've probably always heard a long "E."
Now hearing the "A" sounds rather funny.

3

Yes, there is a small fact that you may not know.
The Easter bunny wasn't always called so.
His mother gave him the grand moniker
Of Mr. Edward Albertson Ster.

After he was an adult and full grown,
E.A.Ster is how he came to be known.
Over time the "E" was all you could hear,
Since people don't really speak very clear.

The bunny was a creative soul.
To make the world brighter was his goal.
He painted his house in colors galore.
He even painted the ceiling and floor.

One fine Spring day, he was roaming about,
Feeling especially joyful, no doubt.
"Mr. E.A.Ster bunny extraordinaire,"
He sang as he wiggled his derriere.

He wanted to give and to share all his joys,
But Santa was already giving out toys.
He looked around with artistic eye,
And snow white hen's eggs his eyes did spy.

"Perhaps I can paint those the colors of flowers.
That's something I'd enjoy doing for hours,"
The bunny pondered this to himself,
Then took his paints down off of the shelf.

The eggs were a breathtaking sight to behold.
They shimmered in pastels and silver and gold.
"Children would surely dance, sing, and shout,
If they saw these beauties lying about."

He scattered them in the yard of a house,
Ignoring the curious eyes of a mouse.
Then a super idea popped into his mind,
"What if I hide the eggs for kids to find?

Children love to play hide and go seek.
A basket of eggs to find would be a treat."
He thrilled at the giving and mystery,
And the rest, you well know, is history.

Now that you know the true E.A.Ster story,
Dasher's still talking, so we'd better hurry
Back to the reindeer to listen in
And hear what it is they're about to begin.

"He likes to hide gifts and so do we.
Why not infringe upon his spree?
We could start a Spring reindeer present.
Kids could find this tradition quite pleasant.

We have this reindeer gift hiding thing down,
And giving gifts is the best fun we have found.
This could become a new reindeer Spring habit.
Santa was clueless so why not the rabbit?"

Again, Dasher held out all of the straws.
This is one of the gift hiding laws.
It's the fairest way to determine first honor.
Wouldn't you know it, again it was Donner!

Donner ran and grabbed a gift from the stash
And was back from the house in a super quick flash.
But it's true that he isn't as smart as a fox.
He carelessly hid a Christmas wrapped box.

The bunny was surprised to see
A Christmas gift under a tree.
"What is the meaning of this thing?
Christmas gifts aren't found in Spring!"

He thought that act was rather brash
And threw the gift right in the trash.
The reindeer saw what he had done.
E.A.Ster had deftly won.

Of course a gift in Christmas paper
Would stick out in this Springtime caper.
They should leave an unwrapped toy
For every little girl and boy.

Blitzen raced off in a blur
And hid a gift in some larkspur.
But that bunny found it since he's clever.
"An unwrapped toy among eggs? Never!"

This too was tossed out with great haste.
Time was a thing he did not waste.
The deer were nearly at wits end.
Did Spring and reindeer just not blend?

Then Prancer thought of something better.
"Why not hide a reindeer letter
To tell each kid how they are special?
This surely would be beneficial.

Kids need to hear this fairly often
Or hopes and dreams begin to soften."
The deer were glad this thought occurred,
And Dasher penned some caring words.

Prancer slid the letter under a rose,
But that bunny had one uncanny nose.
He sniffed out that letter before you could say,
"Jack Rabbit" and quickly threw it away.

The deer sat around fairly discouraged.
Then Comet had an idea they encouraged.
"What if we find a reindeer gift way
For our gift to blend with the bunny's gift day?"

Comet blazed off with glorious speed
(He is the fastest reindeer indeed),
Then was back inside the blink of one eye,
Leaving the bunny wondering why.

He didn't see any change in what he had hid.
He tried figuring out what the reindeer did.
But try as he might, he couldn't guess.
The reindeer gift looked like the rest.

He hopped and he looked for the reindeer joke,
But he could not find the hoax to revoke.
Now the sun was climbing high in the sky.
It was time for the bunny to say good-bye.

But he was still as curious as could be,
So he hid by a bush and waited to see.
The children came pouring out into the yard.
Spotting bright bunny eggs wasn't too hard.

One girl picked up an egg that looked funny.
It looked unfamiliar to E.A.Ster bunny.
She stopped and looked at the egg in her hand.
Around the center there was a thin band.

She popped the egg open and held up her prize.
Mr. E.A.Ster bunny rubbed at his eyes.
There in her hand held high to be seen
Was a miniature reindeer figurine.

Now that he knew just how he'd been had,
He promised this deer gift would be but a fad.
But the deer had great fun with their Spring gift rendition
And equally promised a new Spring tradition.

So now that you know this tale true,
Will the reindeer hide a Spring gift for you?
Or will E.A.Ster bunny win the game
And protect his Springtime egg hiding name?

Does the bunny or deer win this Spring tradition?
Each year starts a new, Springtime competition.
Go to www.reindeergift.com,
And vote for which one you want your gift from.

The Author

Elizabeth Passo has always had a happy knack for rhyme and stories and impulsively bombards her friends and family with her imaginative creations. After hearing how much you loved the unique looks and personalities she and artist Jon Carraher developed for each of Santa's 8 beloved reindeer in her first book, <u>The Reindeer Gift: A fun, easy Christmas tradition</u>, Elizabeth was inspired to continue the reindeer caper. She lives in central Pennsylvania with her two number one fans as well as a not quite perfect but beautifully golden and rosy nosed pit bull and a gargantuan pussycat. She'd love to hear from you! You can learn more and contact her at *elizabethpasso.com* or *www.reindeergift.com.*

The Artist

Jon Carraher has an imagination that runs wild and loves sharing his mind through many forms of art. He is always busy with new creations and ideas that never seem to stop flowing. After working on their first successful project together, <u>The Reindeer Gift: A fun, easy Christmas tradition</u>, Jon and Elizabeth decided to continue the great author/artist team to bring you this enjoyable sequel. Jon lives in central Pennsylvania with his wife Kyra, and their extra friendly cats. You can see more of Jon's artwork and contact him at:
www.joncarraherartworks.com

ORDER FORM

MAKE PAYABLE TO:
Happy Knack Publishing, LLC
MAIL TO:
70 Squirrel Hill, Milroy, PA 17063

INTERACTION	PRICE	QTY	TOTAL
The name of the reindeer that hid your Christmas gift this year	FREE		
Vote for the Springtime competition and find out the winner	FREE		
Shipping and Handling (Add $1.00)			
INTERACTION TOTAL			

BOOKS	PRICE	QTY	
THE REINDEER GIFT Hard Cover Book	$24.95		
THE REINDEER VS E.A.STER Hard Cover Book	$24.95		
The Reindeer Hard Cover Book Set (10% Discount)	$44.90		
Gift Wrapped Book - Specify Christmas or Birthday (Add $1.00 Each)			
Shipping and Handling			FREE
BOOK TOTAL			

MY FAVORITE REINDEER IS... 4"x5" STICKERS	PRICE	QTY	
Dasher	$2.00		
Dancer	$2.00		
Prancer	$2.00		
Vixen	$2.00		
Comet	$2.00		
Cupid	$2.00		
Donner	$2.00		
Blitzen	$2.00		
Shipping and Handling (Add $1.00)			
STICKER TOTAL			

REINDEER GIFT CARDS	PRICE	QTY	
Pack of 8 Christmas cards - 1 of each reindeer plus envelopes	$21.00		
Pack of 8 All Purpose blank cards - 1 of each reindeer plus envelopes	$21.00		
Shipping and Handling (Add $2.50)			
CARD TOTAL			

ORDER SUBTOTAL			
Sales Tax (PA residents add 6%)			
ORDER TOTAL			

SHIP TO:		PAYMENT INFORMATION:			
Name		**Card Type**	Visa	Master	Other (Specify)
Address		**Card #**			
		Expiration Date			
		Validation Code			
*Phone #		**Name on Card**			
Email		**Signature**			

*Please print very clearly and be sure to include your correct phone number in case we have any questions or problems processing your order. We do not sell or give out personal information.

Checks and money orders are also accepted at the address above

For PayPal payments, email us at sales@reindeergift.com